THE CHILDREN'S CLASSICS Collection

Dados Internacionais de Catalogação na Publicação (CIP) de acordo com ISBD

B964t Burnett, Frances Hodgson
The secret garden / Frances Hodgson Burnett. - Jandira, SP : W. Books, 2025.
120 p. : 12,80cm x 19,80cm. (Clássics).

ISBN: 978-65-5294-122-0

1. Literatura inglesa. 2. Clássicos. 3. Aventura 4. Sonho. 5. Amizade. 6. Órfão.
I. Título. II. Série.

2025-2478 CDD 820
CDU 821.131.1

Elaborada por Lucio Feitosa - CRB-8/8803
Índice para catálogo sistemático:
1. Literatura inglesa : 820
2. Literatura inglesa : 821.131.1

Text based on the original story by Frances Hodgson Burnett,
adapted by Gemma Barder
Illustrations by Rebecca Price

1st edition in 2025
www.cirandacultural.com.br

The Secret Garden

Frances Hodgson Burnett

W. Books

Mary Lennox

A young girl

Mrs Medlock

A housekeeper

Martha Sowerby

Mary's maid

Dickon Sowerby

Martha's brother

Colin

A sick young boy

Mr Craven

Mary's uncle

Ben Weatherstaff

A gardener

Chapter One

Mary Lennox was ten years old and had never had a friend.

To make matters worse, her parents never spent any time with her; her father was busy with work, and her mother preferred to spend time attending glamorous parties.

The family lived in a grand house in India, far away from any of their relatives. Mary's only companions were the servants.

She only knew how to give orders. In short, she was miserable.

One morning, when Mary awoke, instead of opening her eyes to see her breakfast laid out as usual, she saw that her large bedroom was empty. As she sat up, she was amazed to see that the servants who were usually waiting to dress her were nowhere to be seen. 'Hello?' she called. 'Is anyone there?'

Mary swung her legs out of bed and padded across the marble floor.

She slowly opened her bedroom door and peeked into the corridor. It was definitely morning. It was the middle of summer, and the hot sunshine was already streaming in through the central courtyard of Mary's house.

Usually at this time, plates full of fruit and bread would be hurriedly taken to Mary's parents' room so they could enjoy breakfast in bed, but the courtyard was still and silent.

Although Mary was familiar with not having anyone to talk to, she found the silence in the house unsettling. She crept along the corridor to her parents' bedroom. Ordinarily, she wouldn't have been allowed anywhere near it. She saw her parents for a few moments each day after dinner, and that was all. She never spent any time in their bedroom and would never call out for them in the night.

Through the door she could hear people talking in panicked voices. 'There is nothing we can do,' said a voice. 'The disease has taken hold of them.'

Mary stepped back when she heard footsteps approaching. She crouched behind a marble pillar as two men in white linen suits left the room. 'The whole house has been taken ill,' said one of the men. 'We must tell everyone not to come here. Cholera has swept through this place.'

As soon as the men were gone, Mary walked slowly back to her bedroom and got back into bed. She had heard the word 'cholera' before. It was a terrible disease.

Mary lay down and pulled her bed sheets up to her neck. She

didn't know what else to do. For hours, she lay and watched the thin net curtains that surrounded her bed float in the Indian breeze. Her stomach rumbled, but even if she knew *how* to make herself something to eat, she had no idea *where* the kitchen was.

After what felt like many hours of waiting, Mary decided to go into the garden. It was the only place in the whole house that gave her any joy.

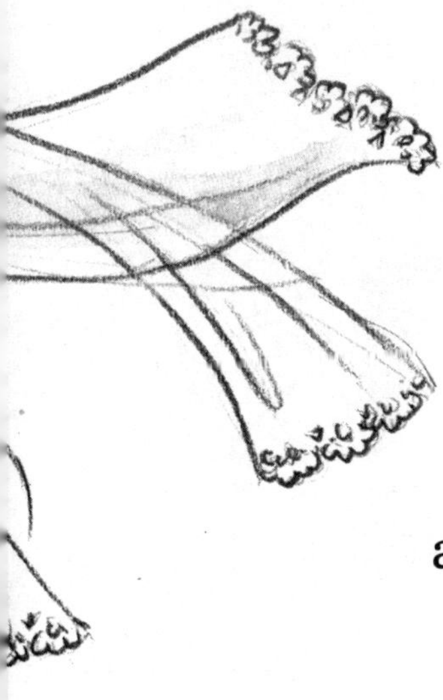

She was walking around the brightly coloured flowerbeds, when she heard the distant voices of men shouting instructions. ‘Who are you?’ said a man in a smart uniform, his shining buttons and medals glinting in the sunlight. ‘And what are you doing out here in your nightdress?’

Chapter Two

The man who had found Mary in the garden was an army officer. He was also the person who took Mary away from the house and told her that both her parents had died of cholera.

He was amazed when the young girl didn't cry when receiving the news. Mary had simply nodded and thanked the army officer for telling her. She couldn't tell him that she barely knew her parents;

it seemed shameful somehow, not to cry at their deaths.

That afternoon, Mary was taken to a large building with floors of offices. She sat on a hard, wooden chair as women in smart clothes tapped away at their typewriters and talked in hushed voices. 'I didn't even know the Lennoxes had a daughter!' said one of the women. 'What are we going to do with her?'

Mary was given a sweet bun to eat, and she realised just how hungry she was. When the army officer returned, she hoped it was to give her another one, but instead he knelt down and spoke to her in a soft, kind voice. The type of voice Mary was not used to hearing. 'You are going on an adventure,' he said. 'Your uncle has a large house in England, and he has agreed that you can go and live with him. What do you say?'

Since Mary knew she didn't have a choice in the matter, she simply asked: 'Are there any more buns?'

The trip from India to England was long and exhausting. Mary kept a file of documents with her at all times. On each part of her journey, they were checked

and signed by a grown-up. Some grown-ups were kind, some were too busy to be kind, but Mary didn't mind. She wanted the journey to be over. And after a long trip at sea, followed by three different trains, it was.

Finally, Mary was in England. She exited the train and stood in the cold on the railway platform.

Mary noticed it was much colder here than in India. She felt goosebumps prickle her skin.

She watched as the rest of the passengers made their way out of the station, until there was one tall, pale-looking woman left.

'Are you Miss Lennox?' said the woman. She was wearing a long grey dress and her hair was pinned up so tightly Mary was certain it must have been hurting her head.

Mary nodded in reply. 'Right then. I'm Mrs Medlock,

your uncle's housekeeper. You are to come with me. Where are your things?'

'I don't have any,' replied Mary. 'I was not allowed to bring anything from my house in India in case I brought the cholera with me.'

Mrs Medlock stared at the young girl. 'Well, we don't get much of that round here,' she said. 'Follow me.'

Mrs Medlock walked quickly and without looking back to see if Mary was following. They walked out of the train station and Mrs

Medlock opened the door to a large black carriage. 'Up you get, we don't have all day,' she said.

On their journey, Mary finally had the chance to look around at her new home in England. She had never seen so much green in her whole life. The fields were green, the trees were green and the hills, which seemed to go on forever,

were also green. She looked at Mrs Medlock and frowned. She seemed cold and unfriendly. At least the servants who looked after her in India smiled occasionally. 'Where are we going?' asked Mary.

'Misselthwaite Manor,' replied Mrs Medlock. 'And there are some rules you need to learn before we get there.'

Chapter Three

Mary had never met her uncle. She knew she had one, and that he lived in England, but she didn't know what he looked like, what his home would be like or what sort of person he might be.

Mrs Medlock sat upright in the carriage and began to give Mary a full list of rules that her uncle expected her to

live by. 'There will be no running about or making noise of any sort. There are over a hundred rooms in Misselthwaite Manor and Mr Craven has been kind enough to give you one of them,' she said. 'The rest aren't for you to be poking your nose about in.'

'Who is Mr Craven?' asked Mary.

Mrs Medlock frowned at the girl. 'Archibald Craven, your uncle!'

Mary nodded solemnly, realising she hadn't known her own uncle's name.

'He doesn't like to be disturbed,' said Mrs Medlock.

'Why?' asked Mary.

Mrs Medlock stared out of the Carriage window for a moment. 'Well, he's not very happy,' she began. 'His wife passed away ten years ago and he's … well, he's not quite gotten over it.'

Before Mary could ask any more questions, she was taken aback by the sight from the carriage window. They were high up in the hills now and Mary could see nothing but a sea of green tumbling away from her. 'Where are we?' gasped Mary, pressing her nose to the window.

'Missel Moor,' replied Mrs Medlock. 'Now sit still, we'll be at the manor soon.'

Misselthwaite Manor was a large, grey stone house. It looked like a castle from one of Mary's books and it was nothing at all like her house in India. Large stone steps led up to a big wooden doorway that was opened by an old man in a tailcoat and bow tie. 'Here she is,' said Mrs Medlock.

'Is Mr Craven ready for her?'

'Mr Craven is busy and must not be disturbed,' said the old butler. 'The young miss is to go straight to her room.'

Mary saw a brief look of frustration cross Mrs Medlock's face. 'Follow me then,' she said to Mary.

Inside the manor was not much warmer than outside. When she had left India, it had been hot and sunny, and Mary shivered in her thin dress as her footsteps echoed on the stone floor.

They walked up a huge wooden staircase and down another corridor. Mary gazed at the paintings on the wall as she passed. Pictures of the manor, the countryside and then of a little girl who looked just like her. 'That's your mother I believe,' said Mrs

Medlock. Mary was astonished by the fact they looked so alike. She had never thought of her mother as being young before, and for the first time she felt a small pang of sadness when she thought of her.

'Here, now don't make a fuss, I'll send up some tea then you're to go straight to bed,' said Mrs Medlock, opening a door to usher Mary inside. The room was large and a small fire had been lit. A four-poster bed sat in the middle of the room and two narrow windows let in a gloomy light. As she stood on her tiptoes, Mary could just see Missel Moor through them.

Chapter Four

When Mary awoke, she thought she was back in her old room in India. As she rolled over and saw the thick red curtains of her bed, she remembered where she was.

A short knock on her door was followed by a young maid carrying a tray. 'Morning, miss,' she said cheerfully. 'I've brought your breakfast.' She set the tray down on a small table by the fire and drew the curtains to let the light in.

Mary watched the girl bustle around the room.

'Shouldn't I get dressed first?' asked Mary. After all, it was the first thing she did in India.

'If you like,' said the maid, opening the tall wardrobe. 'Mr Craven had these sent for you, so I hope they fit.'

Mary gazed at a set of dresses in heavy fabrics that were hanging in her wardrobe. 'These are for me?' she asked, disbelievingly.

'Well, they sure as anything aren't for me!' laughed the maid.

'I'll wear that one,' said Mary, pointing to a green woollen dress.

She stared at the maid. The maid stared back. 'What are you waiting for?' said Mary. 'I said I would wear that one.'

The maid frowned in confusion. 'You want me to help you get dressed?' she asked.

'Of course, that's what servants do!' said Mary.

'You mean you have never dressed yourself before?' asked the maid, shocked.

Mary looked down at her feet. Apart from on the boat over from India, Mary had never had to dress herself. She felt her cheeks go red with embarrassment.

'It's all right, miss, I'll get you sorted out. My name's Martha,' she said, unhooking the dress from its hanger and throwing it on the bed. 'Watch what I'm doing, mind, as

I won't have time to dress you every day.'

Once the dress was on, Mary smiled at Martha. 'Thank you,' she said. 'What shall we do now?'

Martha laughed. '*Now* I have to get back to work!' she said, straightening Mary's bed and picking up her washing from the floor. With that, she left the room and Mary was alone once again.

Mary wandered through the great house. Her footsteps echoed through the giant, empty reception rooms. She hovered outside her uncle's office, but dared not enter.

Soon she found herself in a garden. It was a large, square garden surrounded by high brick walls. The flowerbeds were arranged in neat rectangles with signs displaying what was being grown there. Although it was nothing like the brightly coloured garden she had in India, Mary

couldn't help but smile at the wealth of plants and vegetables on display.

Just then, a small bird with a bright red chest fluttered so close to Mary that for a moment she thought it was going to land on her. 'Don't worry, miss!' said a gruff voice. 'That's just Mr Robin.'

Chapter Five

Ben Weatherstaff had been the gardener at Misselthwaite Manor for so long, he remembered the day Mr Craven was born. His hair and beard were white, and his face was weathered. 'I've never seen a robin before,' said Mary, following the little bird as it hopped from plant to plant.

'Never seen a robin?' chuckled

Ben. 'Where've you been living? Under a rock?'

'No,' replied Mary politely. 'India.'

'Well now, I imagine there's quite a lot round here you haven't seen before,' said Ben, kneeling down to work on the vegetable patch in front of him.

'That's true,' replied Mary. 'Can you teach me what some of these plants are?'

Ben looked up at the small girl in her neat clothes. 'These are vegetables, miss. This is the kitchen garden and through that arch you'll find the rest of the grounds.'

Mary nodded solemnly, but did not move. Ben knew enough about the sad history of Misselthwaite Manor to know that Mary's days wouldn't be filled with much excitement. 'All right,' he said. 'You can help me pull up these weeds.' Ben patted the little cushion next to him. 'And don't you be worried about old robin there. He comes every year to keep me company.'

Mary stared at the dark brown soil and frowned. She had never pulled weeds, or done anything at all that could be considered as work.

'Very well,' she said.

Mary spent the rest of the morning following Ben around the kitchen garden while he told her the which of the little sprouting plants were weeds, and which were vegetables.

Her hands turned brown with dirt, but Mary didn't mind. She liked the smell of the soil and the feel of the cool morning air on her cheeks.

As Mary gathered her basket of weeds to take over to the pile Ben called his 'compost heap', Mary heard the stable clock chime twelve. 'That'll be your luncheon, miss,' said Ben. 'I'd be running along if I were you.'

'Thank you, Ben,' said Mary. 'That was most enjoyable.' As Mary made her way out of the garden and back into the house, she realised how good she felt. The fresh air had filled her lungs and as she caught sight of her reflection, she could see that her pale skin was now pink and glowing.

'Where have you been?' said Mrs Medlock, blocking Mary's path back to her room. Mary quickly put her muddy hands behind her back.

'Just for a … a walk in the gardens,' replied Mary.

'Young ladies must be present in the dining room at twelve sharp, unless you'd prefer to skip lunch altogether …' Mrs Medlock stopped talking to stare at Mary's dress. 'What have you done to yourself? There's mud all over you!'

Mary reached down to grab the edge of her dress and as she did, Mrs Medlock saw, with horror, the state of Mary's hands covered in dirt.

Mary's face turned red and she opened her mouth to speak when something stopped her. A strange tearful cry could be heard coming down the corridor. 'What's that?' asked Mary, confused.

Mrs Medlock straightened up. Her face was emotionless. 'Nothing. It's absolutely nothing. Get to your room, clean up and be in the dining room in ten minutes or I'll tell the cook to give your food to the dogs.'

Chapter Six

It had been two weeks since Mary had arrived at Misselthwaite Manor and she still hadn't been introduced to her uncle. Now, Mr Craven had gone away on business.

Mary didn't mind, however. She was used to grown-ups ignoring her, so nothing seemed out of the ordinary. In any case, Mary had found something she enjoyed. Being outside.

On the days when Ben was working in the kitchen garden, Mary would tag along by his side, asking him questions, filling his watering can or digging about in the soil. Occasionally the little robin would sit on a bush nearby and watch them as they worked.

On other days, Mary had taken to going for walks on Missel Moor. She loved looking over the fields and watching the grass sway in the wind like waves on a beach. Each night she fell into a deep sleep, her legs and arms aching from being more active than she had ever been before.

Then, the rain came. 'Cheer up, miss,' said Martha as she laid out a small tray of tea and cake for Mary in her room.

'But I wanted to explore the gardens some more,' sighed Mary.

'No doubt you're looking for the secret garden,' said Martha.

Mary jumped up from the window seat where she had been watching the rain pour over the moor. 'Secret garden?' she asked.

Martha smiled. 'My mum says

it belonged to Mr Craven's wife,' she said, almost whispering, afraid that someone might overhear. 'She loved roses and all kinds of different flowers, so she built the most beautiful garden. Then, when she died, Mr Craven locked the door and threw away the key!'

Mary was fascinated by the story for two reasons. First, she was desperate to find out if there really *was* a secret garden in the grounds of the manor, and second, she wanted to know more about Martha's mother.

'Does your mother talk to you often, then?' asked Mary.

Martha smiled. 'Of course!' she said. 'She's the first person I speak to when I wake up and the last person I speak to at night. She's my mother!'

'I never really spoke to mine,' said Mary simply. 'I don't think

she liked me very much. In fact, I don't think adults like me very much at all.'

Martha's smile faded and she threw her arms around Mary. Mary stiffened. She had

never been hugged and she was not sure what she should do, but after a moment, she put her arms around Martha and hugged her back, feeling her warmth and comfort.

'It's got nothing to do with you, miss,' said Martha, almost angrily. 'That's not how *real* families are supposed to behave.'

'What's your family like?' asked Mary.

Martha smiled. 'There's me, my dad, my mum and my younger brother Dickon. Dickon is like you, he likes to be outside. He helps my dad look after the horses, but he's always got some animal or other trailing after him. Dad says he's got a magic touch.'

Mary was amazed by Martha's story of her family. She wished that she could stay and talk some more. In truth, she wished she could go home with Martha and be part of her family, instead of the one she was born into.

Chapter Seven

The following day, Mary was overjoyed to see that the rain had stopped. She ate her breakfast quickly, then she got dressed all by herself – as she had now learnt to do.

She was desperate to get into the gardens and explore. Mary had been dreaming all night about finding the door to the secret garden and wondering what could be inside. She ran through the kitchen garden, waving to Ben, but not stopping, and out into the beautifully kept formal gardens, with its rows of box hedging and flowers.

Mary knew the secret garden would be somewhere out where the garden turned into a wilderness, where trees and ivy battled for space among the old garden buildings.

Mary ran her hand along an old brick wall, feeling for a door or archway, but discovered nothing. 'Oh, Miss Lennox!' said Martha, nearly bumping into Mary head on. 'What are you doing in this part of the manor?'

‘I’m looking for the secret garden!’ said Mary. ‘Why, what are you doing here?’

‘This is the way all the servants come in and out of the grounds. Did you think we used the front door?’ laughed Martha. ‘I’m glad you’re here,’ she said, as she reached into the basket on her arm. ‘I told my mum all about you and, well, she wanted you to have this.’ Martha pulled out a skipping rope with red, wooden handles. ‘She said it wasn’t right that you were all alone up here with nothing to do, so she thought this might help pass the time.'

Mary took the skipping rope from Martha as carefully as if it were the Crown Jewels. 'Your mother gave you this, for *me*?' she asked.

Martha smiled and continued into the house to begin her work, leaving Mary to stare at the rope. Martha's mother had never even met Mary before, and yet she was worried about her. It made no sense to Mary, and but made her feel warm and cared for. Was that what it felt like to be part of a real family?

Mary forgot all about her quest for the secret garden as she set about learning to skip. It was tricky at first, but she soon got the rhythm of jumping in time with the rope.

In fact, it wasn't until the rope swung over her head and caught on some thick, overhanging ivy that Mary stopped what she was doing.

As she pulled the rope free, a trail of ivy fell and revealed the top of a crumbling, wooden

quest

To go on a difficult search to achieve or find something.

door covered in moss. Mary's heart started to pound. She scrambled to pull the rest of the ivy away from the wall and soon uncovered the rest of the door.

The secret garden! Mary thought, wishing Martha was there to see it too. She rushed to try the rusted, black doorknob, but as hard as she twisted it, the door wouldn't open.

Mary crouched on the floor and brushed aside the leaves and sticks and bits of moss that covered the entrance, desperately searching for a key. It was then she heard the familiar chirruping of the robin.

It was stood on top of the wall, looking down at Mary, curiously. 'It's all right for you,' said Mary. 'You can already see what's inside.'

Just then, the robin fluttered down to a small pile of leaves a few steps away from the door. It hopped about from foot to foot. As Mary approached the bird, she could see something long and metal poking out the top.

Mary's hands trembled as she slotted the dirt-covered key into the lock. It clicked loudly and Mary could feel the door handle loosen in her hands. The door opened with a weary creak of years of being unattended. A decade's worth of leaves and dirt were pushed aside to let Mary enter.

As she stepped inside, Mary gasped. The garden was surrounded by high brick walls with ivy and vines that covered nearly every brick. There was a path hidden by crunchy leaves and slippery moss that stretched out in front of her toward a fountain that had stopped flowing years ago.

What Mary liked the most, however, were the roses. Somehow, they were still in bloom all over the garden. White, red, pink and yellow rose buds dotted among the overgrown bushes and flower beds.

The air smelt sweet and was soft on Mary's face. She breathed in and closed her eyes for a moment. When Mary opened her eyes again, the robin fluttered past her happily, and Mary grinned at him gratefully for helping her find the key.

Dappled sunlight fell across the fountain to reveal paths that led in different directions. Mary followed one that took her to a white, metal swing. Although it was rusted in places, Mary swept away the dirt from the seat and hopped on, feeling happier than she could ever remember being in her entire life.

Mary soon spotted the plants that Ben had taught her were weeds and she began to pull them out of the ground. Once she had seen one, she could see more and more and soon she had weeded a whole flower bed.

That's better, she thought, as she stepped back to look over her work. She moved onto the next flower bed, and the next, pulling up weeds and dead plants wherever she could find them. She found an old wheelbarrow propped up against the wall and filled it with waste. She couldn't see a compost heap like the one Ben had in the kitchen garden, so she decided to start one herself. By the time the clock chimed for lunch, the heap was as high as her shoulders.

That evening, as Martha filled a bath full of soapy water, Mary couldn't stop talking about the garden. 'There's a swing, too! Did I mention the swing?' she said.

'You did, yes,' replied Martha.

'And the fountain will be so pretty if I can get it working again, and there are so many flowerbeds but most of the plants have died, apart from the roses and …' Mary paused. 'Maybe I could grow some new plants?'

Martha helped Mary into the

bath. 'That sounds like a fine plan, miss,' she said. 'But you better not mention it to Mrs Medlock. If Mr Craven finds out …'

'He won't,' said Mary, feeling determined. 'Not if I have some help. What about Dickon! Would he help me?'

Martha smiled, knowing her brother would jump at the chance of seeing inside the secret garden. 'I'll ask him,' she said.

Chapter Eight

Dickon Sowerby was younger, but already taller than his sister. He had sandy-coloured hair and a warm, smiley face with big, brown eyes. 'These are for you,' he said, handing a heavy canvas bag to Mary as they stood outside the door to the secret garden. 'Me sister says you're always coming in with dirt stuck in your fingernails, so this'll help.'

Mary peered inside the bag to see a small spade, a gardening fork and a pair of thick gloves. 'Thank you,' said Mary, once again overwhelmed to discover that someone else had been thinking about her welfare. She could feel her cheeks beginning to flush, so she straightened up and cleared her throat. 'Before we go in, I must ask you to swear you will keep this garden a secret from everyone,' she said in a stern voice.

welfare

Somebody's state of well-being and health.

'Aye, aye, captain,' said Dickon, smiling.

Good,' replied Mary. 'Follow me.'

She slipped the key out of her dress pocket and opened the door to the garden. She smiled as she saw Dickon's face light up. 'Crikey,' he said, spinning round to take in every inch of the garden. 'It's fantastic!'

'It is, but we can make it even better. Come on!' Mary ran towards the corner of the garden she had already started to clean. Dickon rolled up his sleeves and picked up the wheelbarrow and together they worked on clearing the paths and weeding the beds.

It took a lot less time with two, and Mary found that she enjoyed being in Dickon's company. He spoke to her in a way that no other child had before. He made her laugh and the time passed

so quickly that when the clock rang out once more, Mary was thoroughly disappointed. 'Will you come again tomorrow?' she asked, fearing that Dickon might say no.

'Of course, miss,' he said.

'Would you mind calling me Mary?' she asked. 'I think we are friends now, after all.'

'Right you are, Mary,' said Dickon. 'Friends it is.'

Since Mary had discovered the secret garden, it was all she could think about from the moment she opened her eyes in the morning.

The best days were days when Dickon could come and help her, but even when he couldn't, she was happier than she had ever been in India.

One particular morning, however, she didn't wake to the sound of birds chirruping outside her window, or Martha coming in to open her curtains. Instead, she woke to hear the distant crying she had heard a few weeks earlier.

She sat upright in her bed. She heard it again. It sounded too young to be Mrs Medlock. Perhaps it was Martha? But that idea was soon squashed when Martha herself came into the room. 'Good morning, miss, awake already?' she said, opening the curtains.

'Martha, who is that who keeps crying all the time?' asked Mary.

Martha turned pale. '*Crying?*

I can't hear any crying,' she replied.

At that moment, the crying got louder and Martha glanced at Mary's door. 'Ha! You *can* hear it!' said Mary. 'Who is it?'

Martha busied herself by opening Mary's wardrobe and pulling out a smart dress. 'You don't have time to be worrying about that this morning, Mr Craven has come home and he wants to see you.'

Mary stood outside her uncle's office door. She was dressed in her best dress and her hair had been neatly combed. She knocked gently and a deep voice told her to enter.

Her uncle was tall, thin and pale. Mary was startled to recognise her own mother in the shape of his eyes, although his hair was dark, while her mother's had been light.

'Come here, Mary,' he said as Mary stepped uncertainly into the room. 'I have been told that I have

been careless in leaving you to your own devices for so long,' he said. He looked uncomfortable talking to her, as though she were an alien from another world. 'Mrs Sowerby, Martha's mother, sent me a note to say that I have been ignoring you, and I suppose that's true.'

'That's quite all right, Uncle, my mother ignored me too,' said Mary, as simply as if she were talking about the colour of the sky.

Mr Craven cleared his throat and frowned. 'I am not used to speaking to small children, but I can see that I should have taken better care of you. So, what would you like?'

Mary looked confused. 'What do you mean?' she asked.

'What would you like to make your life happier here?' he said.

Mary thought for a moment. What she would really like is a family, just like the Sowerbys, with a sister like Martha and a brother like Dickon and a mother like Mrs Sowerby. 'I … like gardening,' Mary said at last, and she noticed a strange look pass over her uncle's face.

'You do?' he replied. 'My wife

enjoyed gardening too. I shall ask old Ben to look out for a patch of garden for you, how does that sound?'

Mary couldn't say that she had found the late Mrs Craven's garden and was already transforming it herself. Instead, she nodded. 'Thank you, that sounds lovely.'

Chapter Nine

When a storm hit Missel Moor, there was nothing the residents of Misselthwaite Manor could do but wait until it had passed. Rain lashed at the windows and thunder rumbled over the moor like a stormy wave crashing against the shore.

On days like these, Mary had taken to staying in her room. She would read, or sketch ideas for the garden. Today, however, Mary had started to hear crying again and this time, she was determined to find out where it was coming from.

She checked to make sure Martha and Mrs Medlock were not around before she sneaked down the corridor to where she was sure the noise was coming from.

Mr Craven was once again away on business, so she didn't have to worry about him.

Soon, she was stood at the far end of the house. The crying was coming from behind the door she was now in front of. She knocked, gently, so as not to alert anyone else that she was there. 'Hello? Who's there?' said a child's voice.

Mary was so shocked that another child was in the house that she barged into the room. She was startled to see a boy, about the same age as her, sat in a huge four-poster bed at least twice the size of her own.

He was very pale, with dark eyes and hair. 'Who are you!' demanded the boy. 'How dare you enter my room without permission!'

Mary scowled at the boy. She was not used to being spoken to in such a way. 'I am Mary Lennox and my uncle owns this house, thank you *very* much!'

The boy stared at her with wide eyes. 'Well, *I* am Colin Craven and my father *owns* this house!'

Mary smiled, despite the rudeness of the boy. 'But that means that we're cousins,' she said, her anger melting away from her.

The boy's face softened. 'I suppose that's true,' he said.

Mary bounded into the room and sat on Colin's bed. 'But why haven't I seen you before? I've been here for months! And why are you always crying?'

Colin stared at the girl as though she were a wild animal. 'I'm sick, you shouldn't come any closer or you might make me worse,' he said. 'I have to stay in bed because I'm too weak to walk.'

Mary looked Colin over. 'You don't look sick to me,' she said. 'A bit pale maybe, but that's because you are in here all the time.'

'I'm sick!' said Colin. 'My father said I can't risk leaving this room or I might get worse.'

Mary frowned and looked around the room. There were toy soldiers on the end of the bed and a huge pile of books. 'You should go,' said Colin. 'I don't want to get any sicker.'

'I can assure you, I never get ill,' Mary said, proudly. 'In fact, since coming here I have not had one

assure

To be certain, or to give someone confidence and remove their doubts.

single sniffle. Don't you get bored in here by yourself?'

Colin fell silent and looked down at his bedsheets. 'Sometimes,' he said.

'That settles it, then,' said Mary. 'I shall come and visit you every day. We are cousins after all. We are family, and family should be together, or so I have learnt.'

Chapter Ten

The next day the storm had passed, but the rain remained. Mary waited until she could be sure Martha and Mrs Medlock were busy, then she ran through the house to Colin's room. This time, he greeted her with a big smile and she jumped up onto his bed without being asked. 'What shall we do?' asked Mary.

'We can play with my toy soldiers, or play a board game?' said Colin.

Mary looked around the gloomy room and jumped up to open the curtains. 'Stop!' said Colin. 'The light will damage my eyes.'

'Don't be so silly!' replied Mary, throwing the curtains open so the light flooded the room. Although it was raining, Mary could see Colin sit up a little straighter as his eyes took in the rolling hills of Missel Moor. 'You see, you're

fine! And we can see your soldiers better too.'

Colin smiled as he handed Mary a set of blue soldiers while he kept the red ones. They played together all morning, until there was a short, sharp knock on the door and Mrs Medlock entered with a tray of soup. 'Good gracious!' she

said, nearly slopping the soup out of its bowl. 'What are you doing in here! And with the curtains open! Get out at once, Master Craven is not to be disturbed!'

Mary jumped away from Colin and backed into a corner of the room. She had never heard Mrs Medlock shout quite so loudly.

'No!' said Colin, stopping Mrs Medlock in her tracks. 'Mary is my cousin and I demand that she stays.'

'But, Master Craven, your health? Your father!' said Mrs Medlock. 'You can't risk getting any sicker.'

'I feel quite well, Mrs Medlock,' said Colin. 'In fact, I feel better when Mary is here.'

Mrs Medlock glared at Mary, but

she knew there was nothing she could do. Colin was Mr Craven's son, and as such, she had to do what he asked of her. She set the soup down and headed for the door.

'Please, Mrs Medlock,' said Colin, as she was just about to leave. 'Don't tell my father about this. He would stop Mary from coming and it is the only thing that has made me happy for a long time.'

Mary stared at Mrs Medlock with pleading eyes. Mrs Medlock nodded silently, then left the room.

'Do you really think you are ill?' asked Mary when she was sure Mrs Medlock had left the room.

'Of course, why would you ask such a thing?'

'It's just,' began Mary. 'When I first arrived, I felt a sort of sickness too. I didn't realise it at first, but when I started to help Ben in the gardens and walk on the moors, I felt so much more alive, I suppose. Maybe, that's what you need too.'

From then on, each day Mary would tend to the secret garden, plant seeds and watch them grow.

Then, she would come inside and spend an hour or two with Colin.

She found it easy to talk to him, and when they bickered (which they often did) Mary found that it didn't last long and they were soon laughing together again. Mary imagined that this must be what it felt like to have a brother, and it filled her heart with happiness.

Chapter Eleven

'I reckon I can get it working again,' said Dickon, taking his hand out of the dirty water of the fountain. 'All it needs is a new pump. Me dad'll have one somewhere.'

Mary clapped her hands excitedly. 'It's just what we need to give the garden something extra special,' she said.

'I don't know,' said Dickon, looking around at the roses and the new plants that had started to grow,

'I think this place is pretty special just as it is.'

Mary ran to her favourite spot in the garden, the white swing. Dickon had oiled it so that it swung freely without creaking, and Martha had found a set of old cushions that fitted it perfectly.

From her seat she could see most of the garden. As usual, Dickon had a trail of creatures scurrying about him as he worked to fish out some of the weeds and dirt from the fountain. Mary closed her eyes, letting the spring sunlight warm her face as she sat back in the swing, breathing in the sweet smells of the garden.

'Mary? Mary? Hadn't you ought to be getting back?' Dickon was gently shaking her shoulder as she opened her eyes once more. 'You've been asleep for over an hour.'

'What?' said Mary, jumping up from the swing in a panic. 'Oh my goodness, Colin!'

Mary ran out of the garden and into the house as fast as she could. She ran through the corridor nearly knocking a laundry basket out of Martha's arms. When she reached Colin's room, she was out of breath.

'Where have you been?' asked Colin, angrily. 'I've been waiting and waiting!'

'I … fell … asleep!' said Mary between breaths. 'If Dickon hadn't woken me, I'd still be there now.'

'Where? And who is Dickon?' demanded Colin. 'I thought you and I were friends!'

Mary had had enough of Colin's

temper. 'If you will just calm down for a moment, I'll tell you!' she said, sitting in her usual spot on his bed. 'In fact, it starts with your own mother,' began Mary.

Mary continued to tell Colin all about the secret garden, and Dickon, and how they were transforming it. She described the air, the light and the smells so clearly, that she was certain she could see Colin's eyes fill with tears.

'I … I think I should go there,' said Colin quietly. 'I think I should go to the garden.'

Chapter Twelve

Mary and Colin giggled at each other when they had first told Mrs Medlock of their plan. She was horrified! Both at the fact that Mary had discovered the late Mrs Craven's garden, and that Colin wanted to leave his room.

Colin was sitting in his wicker and wooden wheelchair, a woollen blanket around his knees. 'I don't know why I'm doing this,' said Mrs Medlock as she pushed it through the corridors of Misselthwaite Manor. 'If Mr Craven catches us, Colin and I will both be in trouble, and you'll probably get sent back to India, Mary.'

Mary was sure she would put a stop to both of those things. But she realised Mrs Medlock was fonder of Colin than she had first thought.

When they reached the door to the secret garden, Dickon was waiting for them. 'This is where I leave you,' said Mrs Medlock. 'I've done my bit; the rest is on you.' And with that, she left.

'Dickon, this is Colin. Colin, meet Dickon,' said Mary.

Colin's natural instinct was to scowl at the boy who had kept his cousin from him, but Dickon's wide smile was too infectious to stay angry with, and Colin didn't mind when Dickon began to wheel him inside the garden.

Mary was pleased that it was a bright, sunny day. She could show Colin the garden at its best. Colin was silent as he stared at the plants, the trees and the sprinkling

instinct

A behaviour that animals and humans are born with, such as the need to hide, eat or sleep.

fountain that Dickon had fixed that morning. 'It's … magical,' Colin said in a voice no louder than a whisper.

They stopped by the fountain and Colin peeked inside. 'Fish,' he said.

'Pardon?' replied Mary.

'It's the only thing I can think of to make this place any better,' said Colin, smiling. 'Some fish in the fountain.'

Dickon and Mary laughed as they busied themselves showing Colin the rest of the garden. ''Ere!

What do you three think you are doing?!' said a deep, gruff voice. The three children looked up to see Ben peering over the wall into the garden.

'Mr Weatherstaff!' said Mary, stunned to see the old gardener. 'We're looking after the garden. What are you doing up there?'

'You shouldn't be in there, it's locked up! I only look over now and then to check on the roses. I didn't want Mrs Craven's favourite flowers to go bad,' he said. 'Hang about, aren't you Master Colin?'

Colin looked worriedly at Mary.

'You shouldn't be outdoors! You're too weak to be in any sort of garden,' said Ben.

'Is that so?' said Colin, a hint of annoyance in his voice. 'If I am so weak, then how come I can do this?' Colin threw the woollen blanket to one side and grasped the sides of his wheelchair. He planted

hang about

A different way of saying 'hang on', or 'wait a minute'.

his feet on the ground and, with shaking arms, he began to lift himself out of his seat.

'Colin! You're standing up!' said Mary.

'How is he doing it?' asked Dickon.

'It's the garden,' replied Mary, smiling at Colin. 'It's magic.'

Chapter Thirteen

As the weeks passed, Colin spent more and more time in the garden with Mary, Dickon and Martha (when she could get away from her chores inside the house). At first, he still brought his chair to the garden, but as he grew stronger, he began to walk there all by himself.

He found that he loved digging in the dirt as much as his cousin. Mary asked Ben which of the roses Mrs Craven had liked best, and Colin paid extra attention to the plant, bringing one of its blooms back to his room in secret to look at.

'Father will be back from his trip soon,' said Colin. 'It means I won't be able to come to the garden as often.'

Mary frowned. 'You should show him how well you are now,' she said. 'And it's all because of the garden.'

'I can't,' said Colin, sadly. 'He never told me about this place and now I know why. It was too painful for him to be reminded of my mother. But being here has made me feel closer to her than I ever have before. She died when I was just a baby, you see.'

'I wonder what type of mother she would have been,' said Mary, dreamily. 'A caring one like Mrs Sowerby or … like my mother …'

The friends remained silent for a moment. A gentle breeze surrounded them with warm air.

'Right, that's enough chatter,' said Dickon. 'Let's play a game of tag.'

Mary and Martha were caught first as they couldn't help but

laugh. Dickon was harder to catch. He swerved and dodged, sending Colin running around the garden in good-tempered frustration.

Colin was laughing but the rest of the friends fell silent.

No one in the garden moved. The only sound was the breeze in the trees above their heads. Colin turned around to see why everyone had stopped running and laughing. 'F-Father?' he said.

'My dearest boy,' said Mr Craven. 'My dearest, dearest boy.'

Mr Craven and Colin sat side by side on the swing while Mrs Medlock stood close by with Martha. Next to them, Dickon and Mary were sitting on the ground.

'I was travelling as usual for

business,' began Mr Craven, 'when I had a dream – a dream about your mother. She was standing in

this beautiful place, telling me to come home to you. When I got back, I came straight to your room and you weren't there. Mrs Medlock had no choice but to tell me the whole story. How Mary found the garden, and how you have been growing stronger each time you came here. I was angry at first, I'll admit. But when I came through that door and saw you playing, really playing like a boy your age should, I felt nothing but joy.' Mr Craven wiped a tear from his eye with a handkerchief.

As Colin and his father hugged, Mary got up and walked away. Suddenly, she felt as though the garden was not hers any longer. It had belonged to Mrs Craven, and now it belonged to Colin and his father. She was not part of their story. She was not part of their family. She was alone, again.

'Mary!' said Mr Craven, trotting after her along the path to the fountain. 'Where are you going?'

Mary felt the unfamiliar sting of tears behind her eyes. She was not used to crying. 'I don't belong here anymore,' she sniffed.

Mr Craven placed an arm around her shoulder. 'Mary, of course you do,' he said. 'Without you, none of this would have happened. The garden belongs to the family, your family. *We* are your family now.'

Mary smiled as she hugged her uncle. She had found a family at long last. A family, and a garden all of her own.

Frances Hodgson Burnett

Frances Hodgson Burnett was born in Manchester in 1849. After moving to the United States and settling in Tennessee, Burnett used her skill of storytelling to financially support her family. A clear talent at only the age of nineteen, her first works were published in a British women's magazine. *The Secret Garden* was published in separate parts in *The American Magazine* before being published as a book in 1911. It remains one of Burnett's most notable novels.